Monty
and the
Ocean Rescue

A Plastic Disaster

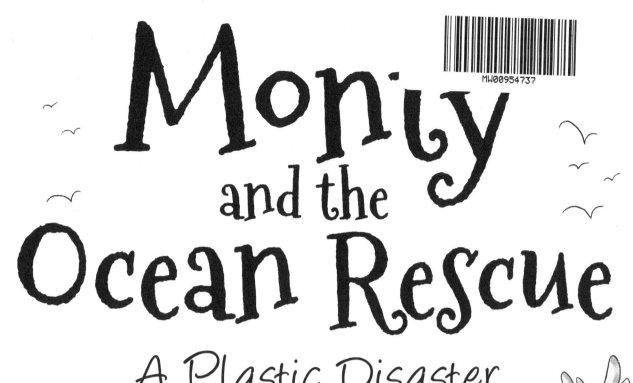

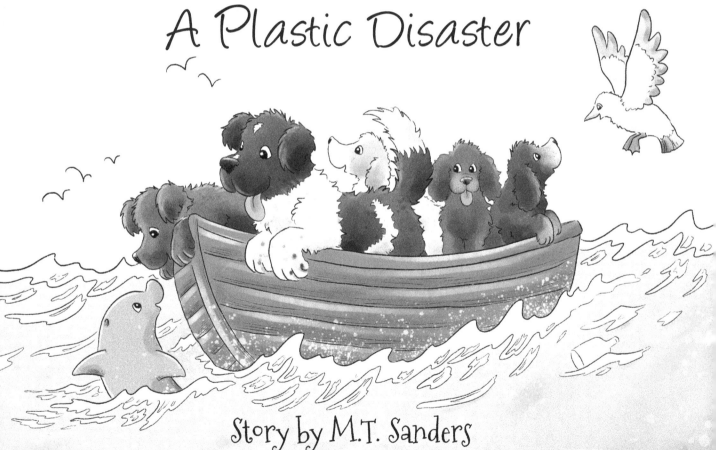

Story by M.T. Sanders
Illustrations by Zoe Saunders

First edition published 2019 by 2QT Limited (Publishing).
Settle, North Yorkshire, BD24 9RH, United Kingdom.

Copyright © M.T. Sanders 2019.

Illustrations by Zoe Saunders.

Printed in Great Britain by IngramSparks.

A CIP catalogue record for this book is available from the British Library.

ISBN 978-1-913071-13-4

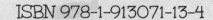

Dedications

This book is dedicated to Sir David Attenborough

I'm sure that everyone will understand why, especially after reading the book. Simply put, here is a man who has inspired so many to take an interest in the beauty of the natural world around them. His passion and infectious enthusiasm continue to enthral young and old alike. In more recent times he has explained the fragility of our planet to the eyes and ears of millions in a way only he can do.

The damage that humans are doing to the worlds fragile ecosystems has never been more important and he has highlighted those issues for all of us to understand. Thank you.

This book is a very small contribution which we hope will raise more awareness about these issues. The hope is to complement the crucial work being done to help our blue planet by bringing this story to children through free school visits. We will be linking our story telling sessions with the groups and organisations who are leading the fight for a cleaner, better planet for future generations.

If you would like more information please contact us through the website at **www.montydogge.com**

This story begins on a warm sunny morning.
We were off to the beach but this time with a warning.

No dragons.
No caves.
No adventures, or quests.

But this sensible advice would give Cookie a test!

It was quiet and calm no-one else was in sight,
when suddenly something zoomed past at full flight.

Straight into the sea Cookie suddenly dashed,
swimming out quickly where she'd seen a big splash.

She was bringing back something
and it looked like a struggle.

Then I had that old feeling;
this was going to be trouble.

So who was it Cookie had swum out to aid?
Were my eyes playing tricks?....

Was that a MERMAID?

Half-hooman, half-fish I knew straight away –
It's not something you see at the beach every day.
A hooge fishing net had been dragging her down.
So Cookie rushed out, fearing that she may drown.

Well, the mermaid was saved that was it, job complete.
The adventure was over and the ending was neat.

But you've guessed it – this story is far from the end.

As we listened to a plea from our newly-found friend.

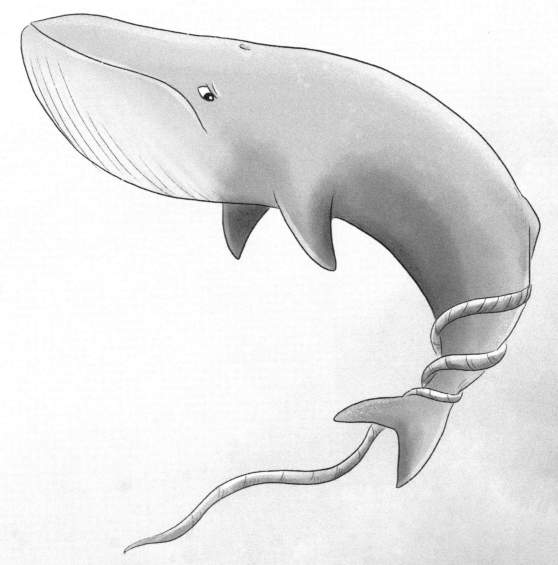

She was on her way South to help a Blue Whale,
who was caught on a rope
that had wrapped round her tail.

But on her way there, she met the same fate.
And now was upset that she'd get there too late.

"We can help!" blurted Cookie,

and I knew straight away
that this was about to be one of those days.

I knew in an instant we must go save the whale –
But we couldn't swim that distance,
we needed to sail.

Bailey had seen a small boat we could use.
So we all clambered on and prepared for our cruise.

But the boat had no motor;
how we'd move wasn't clear.

Then Molly said "I have a brilliant idea."

She jumped up on Bailey,
and Poppy joined the pile.
And the plan that they'd worked out
made everyone smile.

As the wind caught their ears
in this strange doggy tower,
we began to move forward...

With just spangle power!

Our mermaid friend led, and we sailed out to sea.
When we saw a large object –
And wondered what could it be?

It floated in front and we thought we'd collide.
We saw there was a problem as we pulled alongside.

It was a hooge turtle trapped by a plastic-can ring.

He could not swim or move anything!

Suddenly, Cookie dived into the sea.

And twenty bites later the turtle was free.

Now released from the litter, he swam round with glee.
It was lovely to see him so relieved and happy.
He asked to come with us when he heard of our tale –
He wanted to help us to save the Blue Whale.

He even helped pull, which gave the spangles a break.
There's only so much blowing those ears can take.

We travelled at speed but then all of a sudden,
up ahead was a sight – and it wasn't a good one.

On top of the waves lay a dolphin, quite still.
From the way it was floating, it looked really ill.

Wrapped all round her head was a bag made of plastic;
We needed quick action – the situation was drastic.

I could watch it no more it was my time to feature –
I just had to rescue this beautiful creature.

But I jumped out too quickly, I wished I could stop.

Instead of a dive, I did a hooge belly flop.

Everyone had got soaked by my newfdoof wave.
No time to say sorry, there was a dolphin to save.

I tore at the bag and very soon she was free.

But this dangerous litter made me so angry.

Our beautiful oceans are trash filled and it's sad.
I never knew things had got this bad.
But the dolphin was free and she flipped in the air.
We'd helped her escape from her plastic nightmare.

Like the turtle, she wanted to come with us too.
We were happy to welcome her into our crew.
She said she could help, as she could she speak Whale.
I got back in the boat and we returned to the trail.

Now we were close to where the Blue Whale had been.
But we asked lots of seabirds and she hadn't been seen.

Then all of a sudden, the dolphin dived down –
She'd just heard a distant and weak whale sound!

"Help
Me!

Please!

Help..."

When she came to the surface, the news was bad.
The dolphin looked worried and we knew she was sad.

The whale had tired and had slipped deep below.

There was only one chance – so they all had to go.

The turtle and mermaid joined the dolphin to dive.
They needed that rope gone for the whale to survive.

Soon they were back because the rope was stuck fast;
They feared that the chance for a rescue had passed.

I looked at Cookie, and she looked back at me.
And we instantly knew it was our destiny.

To rescue is something that's deep in our soul.

Now me and me sister had only one goal!

Though swimming is natural for us newfydoofs,
deep diving was scary, to tell you the truth.

But we just had to do it, we had to believe
it was just a ginormous underwater retrieve!

We dived deeper and deeper
and soon found the whale.
And we worked with our teeth,
on that rope round her tail.

We ripped, chewed and nibbled, Cookie and me,
and before very long the Blue Whale was free.

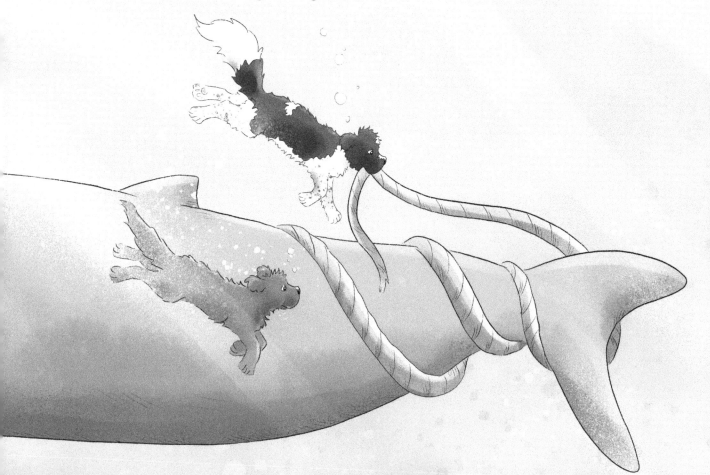

We swam to the surface and got ourselves out,
and the Blue Whale said thank you
with a hooge water spout.

It was time for goodbyes; there were cuddles and tears.
Then we plotted our course and set six spangle ears.

Life went back to normal but I couldn't forget,
about all of that rubbish and our seas under threat.

But news had spread fast
of our deep-water task,
and Mr Attenborough visited
with something to ask.

"Go visit the children and tour lots of schools.
Everyone will listen because Monty is cool.

Look after our planet. Go tell them your tale,
about a small band of heroes
saving the mighty Blue Whale."

Other books available by the author ...

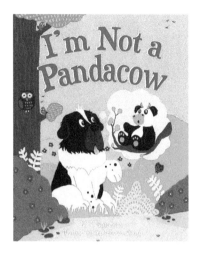

A delightful story about Monty, a huge Newfoundland puppy, and his journey to find out what he is. But will asking the other dogs he meets on his travels give him the answers he wants?

By M.T. Sanders.
With illustrations by Rebecca Sharp.

ISBN 978-1-912014-73

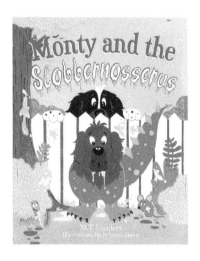

When Monty was asked to look after his new sister how hard could it be? An open gate and a fleeing mailman was just the invitation she needed.
Now it was up to Monty to save the day. So, watch out everyone it's time to run... for your raincoats.

By M.T. Sanders.
With illustrations by Rebecca Sharp.

ISBN 978-1-912014-79-8

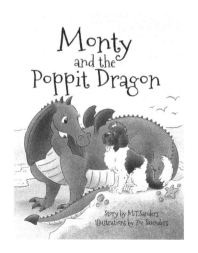

Monty, Cookie and the spangles are off on their holidays to sunny Pembrokeshire and the beautiful beach at Poppit Sands. In a cave they meet a new friend, the Poppit Dragon, who is sad because she can't fly. Can Monty and the gang save the day?

By M.T. Sanders.
With illustrations by Zoe Saunders.

ISBN 978-1-912014-06-4

Other books available by the illustrator ...

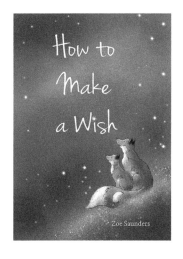

Come on a journey through the countryside as Big Red Fox teaches Little Red Fox how to make wishes. A dreamy children's story with beautiful illustrations, and a heartwarming ending that will leave children feeling loved and cherished, How to Make a Wish is perfect bedtime reading for your little cubs.

By Zoe Saunders.
ISBN 978-1-78808-0385

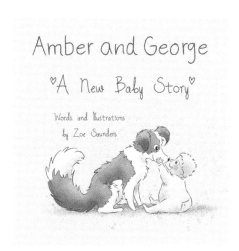

Amber is the dog who has it all. She has a lovely house, a big garden, lots of toys, and she goes for long walks every day. Then one day everything changes. A little baby called George turns Amber's perfect world upside down. But all it takes is a little time and patience for friendship and love to grow.

By Zoe Saunders.
ISBN 978-1-78926-0885

High up in the mountains, far above the clouds, where the Earth meets the sky, there lived a lonely dragon. The dragon embarks on a great journey travelling far and wide in search of a friend, another dragon, just like her. And in the end, she does find true friendship, but not quite in the way she imagined.

By Zoe Saunders.
ISBN 978-1-9164352-0-9

Learn more about how to reduce you plastic waste

If you would like to find out how to reduce your plastic waste, or find out how you can get more involved in the work to protect our sea creatures go to:

https://www.montydogge.com/help-our-oceans

Here you will find some great organisations who will provide more information.

Thank you for being a #oceanrescuer

2QT

PUBLISHING

CPSIA information can be obtained
at www.ICGtesting.com
Printed in the USA
LVHW070528060819
626568LV00023B/2016/P